TROUT THE MAGNIFICENT

Trout

THE Magnificent

BY SHEILA TURNAGE / ILLUSTRATED BY JANET STEVENS

HARCOURT BRACE JOVANOVICH, PUBLISHERS
SAN DIEGO NEW YORK LONDON

For my nieces
Lauren, Karen, and Haven

Printed in the United States of America

Designed by Barbara DuPree Knowles

LIBRARY OF CONGRESS CATALOGING IN PUBLICATION DATA
Turnage, Sheila.
Trout the magnificent.
SUMMARY: Trout, dissatisfied with being an ordinary fish, goes to the animal council to be allowed to fly, but his magnificent adventures in the air lead to unforeseen problems.
[1. Trout—Fiction. 2. Animals—Fiction. 3. Flying—Fiction. 4. Fishes—Fiction.]
I. Stevens, Janet, ill. II. Title.
PZ7.T8488Tr 1984 [E] 82-15865
ISBN 0-15-290962-1

A B C D E
First edition

Once the earth was ruled by a council of animals. Their names were Lion, Owl, Dog, and Ant.

Lion had courage. Owl had wisdom. Dog had love. Ant could do until it was done. Together they ruled the world.

One day Trout came to talk to the council. "I have come to ask a favor," he said.

"What is it, Trout?" Dog asked.

Trout took a deep breath. He scratched his belly. He squirmed. "I . . . I want to fly," he said.

Dog looked at Lion. Lion looked at Ant. Ant looked at Owl. Owl looked at Trout.

"Why?" Owl asked.

"Because," Trout said, "I am short and gray. I have cold beady eyes and a flat clumsy tail. My scales are short and ugly, and I have no ears to speak of." Trout hung his head. "I am an ordinary fish. I don't *want* to be ordinary. I want to be special. I want to fly."

"Trout, you are made for water," Lion said. "You are glorious and brave in the water."

"You have talent and skill," Ant said.

"It's not wise for you to fly, Trout," Owl said. "You're too fat in the middle, and you have no feathers to warm you in the wind."

"You might catch cold," said Dog. "And it hurts to fall from high places, Trout. You just don't *know*."

"I just don't *care,*" Trout said rudely. "I want to fly."

"Well," said Dog, "I want you to be happy, Trout."

"It *would* take courage for a trout to fly," Lion said.

"And a lot of hard work," Ant squeaked.

"It's not wise," Owl said, "but it *would* take know-how."

Lion, Owl, Dog, and Ant looked at each other and shrugged.

"If you insist," Dog said.

"Then you'll give me wings?" Trout cried.

"Oh, no," Ant said quickly. "That's too easy."

Owl stood up and ruffled his feathers. "We will give you a roll of brown paper, two rubber bands, a ball of strong string, eight Popsicle sticks, some glue, and a pair of goggles," Owl said. "If you want to fly, you must build trout wings."

"But . . . " said Trout.

"Take it or leave it," Lion roared.

"I'll take it," Trout said.

And so it was settled.

GLUE

Trout worked day and night to build trout wings. He sketched, erased, and sketched again. He measured, added, and subtracted. He cut, pasted, and tied.

Sometimes Trout grew weary, but each time he was ready to give up, one of the animals came to his rescue. Dog brought a cup of warm milk, or Owl helped him add, or Lion broke something so that Trout became angry and found new energy.

Ant was the most help of all. He beat a twig against Trout's worktable and shouted, "Go for it, Trout," in his squeaky ant voice.

Trout went for it. He stretched the paper tight over Popsicle sticks to make beautiful trout wings. He wove strings to make a strong harness and tied other strings in clever ways so that he could pull them with his fins and make his wings flop. He tied the rubber bands to his harness and draped them over his shoulders, like a general. He dusted his goggles and polished them until they shone.

At the end of three weeks he was ready.

Trout got up early, put on his wings, and tail-vaulted through the forest to the council's house. "Won't everyone be pleased with me?" Trout giggled as he knocked on the door. "I'm here!" he cried as he rushed into the kitchen.

"Have some breakfast, Trout?" Dog asked.

"No," Trout said as he bit into a muffin. "I have something important to do. Today Trout the Magnificent will fly from the highest hill."

"The highest hill?" Owl asked. "Don't you think it would be wiser to try a short tree first?"

"No," said Trout. "The highest hill. I want you all to see."

Lion, Ant, Owl, and Dog shrugged. "All right, Trout," they said. "Good luck!"

Lion, Ant, Owl, and Dog moved their chairs outside and put them in the sun. Trout took a deep breath and started up the highest hill.

The hill was higher than Trout expected, but finally he reached the top.

"Oh, my," he said when he looked down. "This is really very high for a trout." His fins shook as he adjusted his goggles. "Can you see me?" he called.

"Yes," Dog shouted from below. "Do be careful."

"Are you sure this is wise, Trout?" Owl called.

"The ground is a lot farther away than I thought it would be," Trout screamed.

"Brave Trout," Lion roared.

Trout sighed. He had not wanted Lion to say, "Brave Trout."

"I'm going to fly unless someone stops me," Trout called.

"Go for it, Trout!" Ant yelled.

Trout had no choice: he went for it. He stepped back, adjusted his rubber bands, and lay down in the dirt. He tucked his tail close to his fat belly and kicked it out hard. Over and over he kicked—tuck-kick, tuck-kick, tuck-kick— until he was hurtling along the ground, going as fast as a trout ever goes on land.

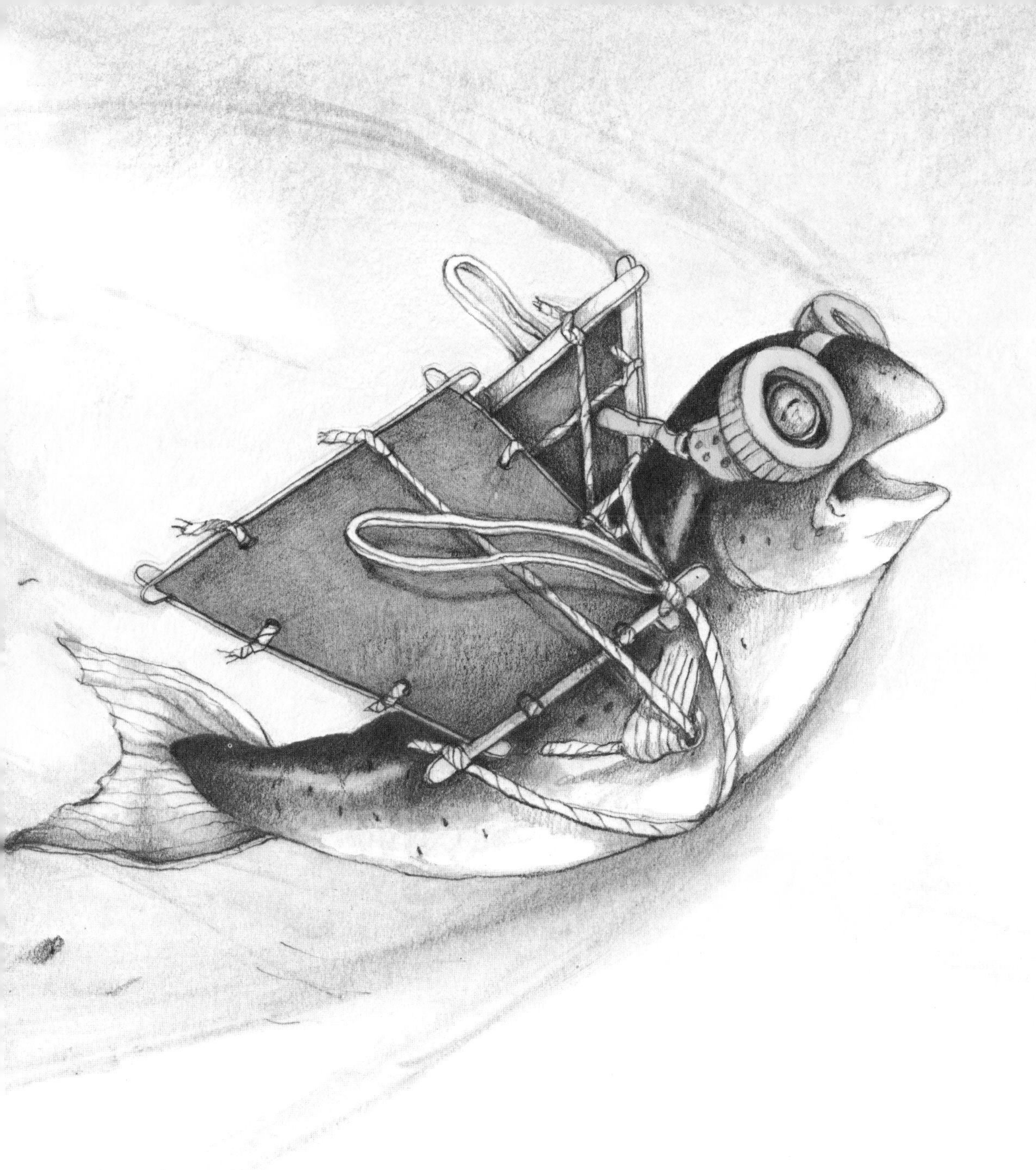

Once he felt the wind whipping across his face, he felt braver. “Won’t this be glorious?” Trout said to himself. “Me, Trout, flying.”

“TROUT THE MAGNIFICENT FLIES,” he shouted as he bounced off the hill. Trout grinned into the wind and pulled his wing-flop strings.

"Oh, no!" Trout screamed as his wings hung limp and his nose pointed down. *"I'm going to get hurt."*

"He's falling!" Owl cried as he soared into the sky and flew toward Trout.

"I'll catch you, Trout," Dog cried as he leaped from his chair.

"Don't look!" Ant told Lion.

"Keep your chin tucked in," Lion roared as he covered his eyes.

"Owl, I'll be sprained," Trout cried as Owl flew up to him.

"Your rubber bands don't work," Owl squawked.

"Don't be stupid, Owl," wailed Trout. "The decorations are the only parts that *do* work."

"What?" Owl said. "Rubber bands aren't for decoration. They're for stretching. Stop and think . . . "

"I can't stop," Trout screamed. "*You* think."

"Idiot fish," Owl muttered. Owl grabbed a rubber band and stretched it to Trout's wing tip. Thwack. The right wing snapped up. Owl stretched a rubber band to the left wing tip. Thwack. The left wing snapped into place.

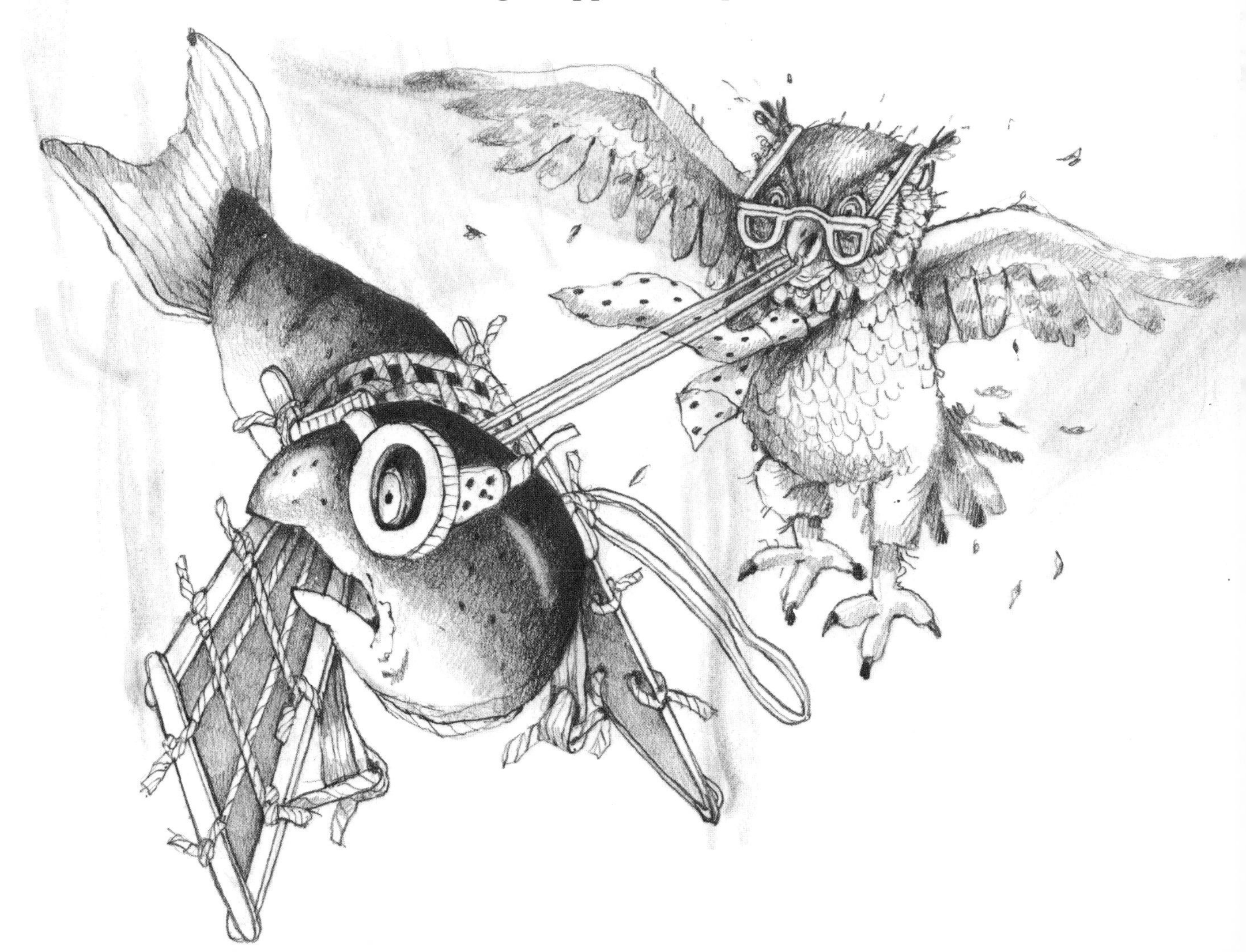

"Heads up, Trout," Dog called from below.

Trout clenched his wing-flop strings, flipped his tail, and pointed his frightened nose skyward. For one second Trout stopped falling.

"Now pull your wing-flop strings," Owl shouted.

Trout pulled. His wings flopped down. Trout stopped pulling. His wings flipped up. He flopped; he flipped. He flipped; he flopped. Up and down he went.

Trout smiled nervously and stretched out on the air. He was flying. "How do I look?" Trout asked.

"You look silly," Owl said. "But you're doing it."

Trout and Owl flew all morning. "It's time to rest," Owl finally called. "We'll land in that cherry tree."

"Roger," said Trout.

Owl pointed his nose at the tree and swooped in low. He pushed his wings up in front and lifted his plump body. He hovered in the air, sank a little, and grabbed the branch with his wrinkled toes. "Now you, Trout," Owl called.

"Roger," cried Trout as he pointed his nose and came in low.

"Slow down!" Dog squealed.
"Not so close!" Lion roared.
"Tilt your wings," Ant hollered.

"Here I am," Trout said when he was close to Owl's head.

Owl moved over to make more room. "Grab hold with your toes," Owl said.

Trout's eyes glazed. *"I don't have any toes,"* Trout shrieked as his belly skidded across the branch.

"Oh, dear," Owl said softly as Trout smacked into the tree.

Dust flew. Cherries flew. Owl flew. Everything flew but Trout. Trout crashed to the ground.

Ant, Owl, Lion, and Dog rushed to him. Dog tenderly removed Trout's goggles and wiped the dirt from his face.

Trout opened one eye. "Am I dead yet?" he asked weakly.

"Not yet," Owl said wisely.

And Dog carried Trout off to bed.

Once Trout was better, Owl taught him to fly without hurting himself. Owl taught him to take off and land without falling. Owl taught Trout to fly in wide, smooth circles and to make short, joyous loops. Owl even taught Trout to glide, so he could rest in the air.

Soon Trout could fly as well as Owl himself. Then the trouble started.

One morning a group of animals hurried through the forest to the council's house. The animals' names were Ostrich, Cat, Deer, and Squirrel.

"Oh, no," Dog said when he opened the door and saw their frightened faces.

"We have to talk to you," hissed Cat.

"It's about Trout the Terrible," whispered Deer.

"Trout the Terrible?" said Dog. "Oh, my!"

"He hides in the bushes," said Ostrich. "He pulls his strings and his wings flop."

"He flip-flops out of the bushes, his eyes wild in the moonlight," said Deer.

"He screams a high, screechy fish scream and dives at our heads," hissed Cat.

"And those goggles!" Squirrel shuddered. "You have to do something. Our children are frightened and our stomachs are upset."

"Oh, my," said Dog. "We'll do something at once."

Owl, Lion, Ant, and Dog found Trout under a bush. "Trout, is it true?" Lion demanded. "Are you frightening the other animals?"

"Yes," said Trout.

"But, Trout . . . why?" asked Ant.

"Because I *want to,*" snapped Trout. "I am the only flying trout in the world. I am special. I can do anything I want."

"No, Trout," said Dog. "You have to remember the others . . ."

"The others don't matter," Trout snarled. "Nothing matters to me except *me*—Trout. Now get out of my way."

Trout stretched out in the dirt and adjusted his goggles. He flipped; he flopped. Trout flip-flopped across the ground and into the sky.

Dog cried. Lion sighed. Ant squirmed. Owl paced.

"I'm going for a walk by Tea Lake," Owl muttered. "Call me the minute that stupid trout returns."

Trout had no intention of returning.

"I don't need them," he said as he flew through a cloud. "I'm not going back. Ever.

"Trout strikes," he screamed, diving at a sparrow and slapping it with his paper wings.

"Trout strikes," he cried as he dove at a robin and stole a worm from its mouth.

"It's Trout the Terrible," the geese honked as Trout flew toward them.

Trout threw back his head and laughed as the geese scattered across the sky.

At that moment a weak, wet voice floated up to him. "Help," it called. *"Help!"*

Trout frowned behind his goggles.

"Trout, help me," the voice cried. "It's Owl. I'm in Tea Lake. I've fallen in. *Save me!*"

"Save yourself, Owl," Trout yelled. "I'm busy."

"Trout, I can't swim," Owl cried.

"*Everybody* can swim, stupid bird," Trout shouted. "Flip your fins."

There was no answer from Tea Lake.

"Owl?" Trout called. No answer. "Stupid bird," Trout muttered. But suddenly Trout felt alone and afraid.

"Owl?" No answer.

"OWL!" Trout screamed as he looked down at Tea Lake. Trout saw only one lonesome brown owl feather floating on the lake. "OWL," Trout cried, "WHERE ARE YOU?"

Trout lowered his head and dove like a wild thing. He burst through breeze and sunshine. He went faster than any living thing.

Trout dove deep into the water looking for Owl. "Oh, Owl," Trout cried as he swam to his friend.

Trout quickly wrapped his left fin around Owl's chest.

"Don't worry," Trout said as he swam to the surface and raised Owl's head out of the water.

"Over here!" Dog cried as he raced toward the lake.

Trout swam to Dog and pushed Owl up on land. Quickly, Trout sat on Owl's back. Trout began pumping Owl's wings back and forth, pushing water out of Owl and air into Owl.

Owl burped. Then he burped again. "Blap!" he said as he opened his golden eyes. "Am I dead yet?"

"Not yet, stupid bird," Trout said. Trout kissed his friend's wet head feathers and smiled.

"What's going on?" Lion demanded as he and Ant ran up to Dog and Trout. "What happened?"

"Trout saved Owl's life," Dog answered proudly.

"Do tell!" said Ant.

So Dog sat up straight and told the whole story.

"Trout, is it true?" asked Lion.

Trout shook his head sadly. "No," said Trout. "Dog left something out. He left out the part where I almost didn't save Owl." Trout hung his head.

"But you *did* come to Owl," Dog said.

"And you dove bravely into the water," said Lion.

"You knew just what to do and you did it," said Ant.

"Oh, anybody can do those things," said Trout. "It's just water stuff."

"*I* couldn't do it," said Dog.

"*I* couldn't do it," said Lion.

"*I* couldn't do it," said Ant.

"*I* couldn't do it," said Owl.

Trout sniffled into his fin. "And just look at my beautiful wings," he cried. Dog gently lifted a blob of brown wrapping paper and Popsicle stick from the lake. "Ruined," cried Trout as he kicked the soggy paper and ripped off his harness. "Ruined."

Trout threw himself into the dirt and rolled about. He knocked his tail against a rock and beat his fins against the earth. "Ruined," he cried. "I'm ordinary again."

Trout lay still in the dirt, trembling, a defeated fish.

"I wanted to be special," Trout said sadly.

Owl lifted himself up on one elbow. "You *are* special, Trout," he said. "You have cold beady eyes, a flat clumsy tail, short grayish scales, and no ears to speak of."

Trout's mouth fell open. "Owl," he howled. "How could you say those things? I thought you loved me."

"I do," said Owl. "I love your beady little eyes that see underwater. I love your flat slick tail that never sinks. I love your invisible ears that don't get caught in your fins when you dive. And those short ugly scales of yours are *not* feathers, Trout. They are not for flying and staying warm in the air. They are *scales,* and they are for gliding through the water like a magic thing when you save owls."

"Oh," said Trout.

"In other words," Owl said as he lay down and closed his eyes, "you are a perfect trout."

"Perfect?" Trout cried. "Me?"

"Perfectly trout," said Dog.

Trout smiled wide.

He wriggled his tail, snapped his fins, and danced a quick fish rhumba.

"Perfect?" he said as he glanced down into the lake.

Trout froze, his fins in mid-snap. "Dog," he whispered, pointing at the lake. "Look at my reflection. DOG, LOOK AT ME!"

"Yes?" said Dog.

Trout peered into the water. "I have colors on me!" he cried. "Look! My scales are beautiful! I must have crashed through a rainbow when I dove to Owl."

"You look the same to me," said Lion.

"I don't see any difference," said Ant.

"You'd never noticed?" asked Dog.

"Why, no," Trout replied. "Who would think something as special as a rainbow would be on an ordinary trout?"

Dog looked at Lion. Lion looked at Ant. Ant looked at Owl.

Owl sat up and looked at Trout. "Me," Owl burped.

Then Owl fell asleep, exhausted.